This book is dedicated to  beautiful beloved, Timothy, my brilliant nephew, Apollo.

I wrote this as a legacy book that can be passed down to the future generations to come. I hope that you will take great pleasure in sharing it with your dearest loved ones.

Edited by: Desirée Monsuraté
Cover image by: Desirée Monsuraté
Book and Cover Design by: Desirée Monsuraté

The Lemon Tree

Written and Illustrated by

Desirée Monsuraté

THIS BOOK BELONGS TO:

_____

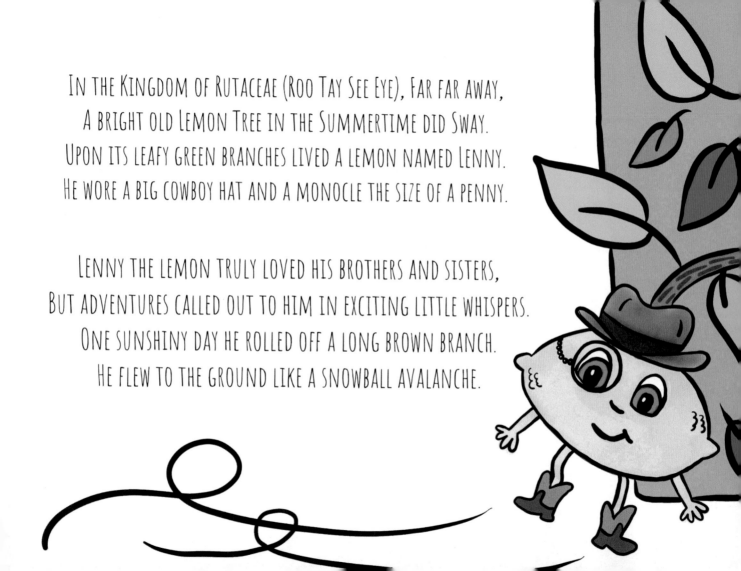

In the Kingdom of Rutaceae (Roo Tay See Eye), Far far away,
A bright old Lemon Tree in the Summertime did Sway.
Upon its leafy green branches lived a lemon named Lenny.
He wore a big cowboy hat and a monocle the size of a penny.

Lenny the lemon truly loved his brothers and sisters,
But adventures called out to him in exciting little whispers.
One sunshiny day he rolled off a long brown branch.
He flew to the ground like a snowball avalanche.

"Goodbye Mother Tree" he called out in a scurry,
"Off I go into the unknown, about me don't you worry"
Mother tree lovingly bid him a giant farewell,
Lenny waved back, and his heart, that day, did swell.

Across wavy hills and Mountains he travelled,
Sometimes his lemon zest simply unraveled.
He'd patch his zest back on with a tender loving pat,
And at night he'd sleep on his yellow yoga mat.

Soon, Lenny arrived at an old wooden hut,
Inside he met an elderly King named Mutt,
King Mutt had wrinkles deep and long,
He said:"Please help, I want these gone."

Lenny was fast to strip a piece off his chest.
"My lemon Treatment for wrinkles works the best."
King Mutt applied the patch to his frown,
And soon that frown turned right upside down.

Lenny the lemon was once again off on his way,
The next place he found was a big barn full of hay.
Outside the barn was a fox scratching her fur.
"These fleas are so pesky, they just won't disappear!"

Lenny quickly peeled her a slice of his arm,
"Here you go Mrs. Fox, this will work like a charm."
Mrs. Fox squeezed the lemon slice onto her back.
Soon, she was itch-free and right back on track.

Lenny tipped his hat and made his way across a stream.
He came upon the most beautiful garden he'd ever seen.
At the table sat Mr. Singh, with a steamy liquid-filled mug.
"I'd love some flavour in my tea; it tastes like an awful bug."

Lenny with a broad smile, gave him a piece of his waist,
"Fear not, my friend, this lemon will flavour your tea in haste!"
Mr. Singh replied, "My tea's alive, there's magic in my cup.
Thank you dear lemon, for dressing my tea up!"

Into a brand new neighbourhood, Lenny stepped with ease,
There he met two siblings who asked, "Will you help us please?'
'Our business is collapsing, our empty cups are sky high.
No one seems to like our drinks and we have no idea why.'

"It just so happens that I have a remedy for the two of you!"
Place some lemon in those cups for a perfect lemonade brew!"
The cups were filled up to the brim, while neighbours formed a queue,
"Your business is thriving,"said Lenny. "I'll bid you adieu."

Lenny was once again, back on his eventful journey,
At a nearby school, Arnold was pacing in a hurry.
"I can't possibly go into class with these pimples galore."
"My friends will start to snicker. They'll laugh at me with a roar."

Lenny squeezed some lemon from his cheek into a cup.
He handed the cup to Arnold and said "Lemon up!"
"Lemon is sure to fade blemishes and even out skin tone!
A cleansing therapy to share with your loved ones at home."

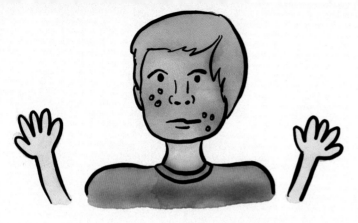

Arnold's face brightened up and so did the skies,
"I won't need to wear a mask."he said. "Not even a disguise!"
"Thank you dear Lemon for this wonderful treat.
Off to school I go, I'm sure glad we did meet."

Lenny sauntered on, with the little lemon body he had left.
He came upon Mr. And Mrs. Messy, sitting on a big golden chest.
"We've searched through all our treasures for an aid to help us clean.
All we want is for our belongings to have that special gleam."

Lenny motioned for Mrs. Messy to lend him her pail,
"With a smidge of lemon in your mix, you simply cannot fail."
"Lemon is an excellent cleaner. It serves just like a bleach."
Sure enough, the new lemon cleaner, found new heights to reach.

Mr. And Mrs. Messy thanked Lenny and went on their way.
Once again, Lenny had been around to save the day.
Now Lenny came upon the finish line of a big exciting race.
Rudolph the runner was panting, a sad frown on his face.

"My toes are a mess. they're all torn and tattered"
Upon his sore feet, calluses and corns were scattered.
Lenny ripped off a chunk of lemon from his thigh.
He graciously offered it to Rudolph, without so much as a sigh.

Rudolph applied the lemon to his aching feet.
In next to no time, he felt as though he were at a spa retreat.
"Thank you dear Lenny, for this magical cure!'
"I can race all over the countryside, it hurts no more!"

When Lenny hopped up to a busy health clinic,
He found patients everywhere that looked rather sick.
One by one, he gave a piece of himself to the crowd,
Vitamin C in their defense cells, made Lenny very proud.

The patients all cheered as they felt good, then great.
A few thanked Lenny for their healthy new state.
Lenny said, "We each have a gift of life to share,
No greater joy fills my heart, than to give with care.

Now Lenny the Lemon was merely a seed.
He stretched and he yawned and soon fell fast asleep.
Lenny woke up the next morning to a shocking surprise.
He had branches and lemons hanging from his new hands and thighs.

The beautiful cycle of life does go on and on,
Lenny was now a gorgeous tree, as bright as the new dawn.
He whispered good morning to his little lemon loves,
The ripest lemon, Lena, flew to the ground like turtle doves.

"Off you go into the world, my darling lemon creation,
You are the joy in my heart, the brightness of this nation."
Lena lovingly hugged her father tree goodbye.
She would, just like Dad, be the answer to a sigh.

COLOUR ME IN!

Lenny's favourite breathing exercises

Smelling Flowers
Imagine you are smelling in a beautiful flower,
breathe in deeply through the nose and out through the mouth.

The bunny breath
Just like a cute little bunny, take three quick sniffs
Through the nose and one long exhale out through the mouth.

Blowing bubbles
Remember how softly you need to blow to get a nice big
Bubble? Take a deep breath in and blow it out soft and long.

Glossary

Rutaceae: is a family, commonly known as the citrus family of flowering plants

Monocle: a single eyeglass

Avalanche: a mass of snow and rocks falling rapidly from a mountain

Scurry: Moving hurriedly with short quick steps

Treatment: a product used in improving the appearance of someone or something

Adieu: a goodbye

Blemishes: small marks or flaws

Disguise: a means of altering one's appearance

Smidge: a small amount

Calluses: a thickened part of the skin

Corns: a small, painful area of thickened skin on the foot

Vitamin C: a nutrient necessary for the growth, development and repair of all body tissues

About the Author

Desirée Monsuraté is a Canadian producer, actor, artist, writer, singer and model, based out of North Vancouver, British Columbia.

Desirée has always had a passionate love for the arts, be it auditory, visual, performance-based or even better, a combination of the above!

Www.Monsurate art.com
Www.Monsurate entertainment.com

Made in the USA
Coppell, TX
17 July 2023